Introduction

The big book of *Yeah! Chinese!* contains various resources, which provides teaching recommendations, strategies, etc. to teach each story and new words.

For teacher's convenience, the big book provides contents as following:

Story's brief introduction helps teachers be familiar with the background of each story beforehand. And teachers can differentiate teaching by expanding more information in details from students' prior knowledge.

Main characters help teachers introduce the main characters to students beforehand and guide students into the story.

Learning objectives are prepared for teachers to set up clear daily goals for students.

New words teaching guides provide teachers with suggestions on the process, strategies and activities of introducing the new words.

Warming up provides suggestions on guiding the students to predict and follow the development of the story.

Story teaching guides provide suggestions and hints to help teachers ask key points of the materials.

Hints such as teaching skills, review activities, classroom management methods, culture elements and the fun points of the stories will help teachers to prepare lessons.

Needed videos (with the logo ▶) during teaching can be found on the official website.

How to use Yeah! Chinese! to teach Chinese?

General guidelines for the procedure of a story lesson

If it is a 3 teaching periods per week, it is suggested to teach with following steps: **First period,** teach new words with song and do the activity about the targeted vocabulary. **Second period,** review the new words, song and predict the cover page of the story; and start the new story. **The last period,** do activities about the targeted vocabulary, and retell the story or do a role play.Teachers may do any changes according to class progress.

Ways to teach new words

• Teach action words such as run, catch, take, etc. with body gestures or movements. For example, when introducing the new word "run", the teacher runs at same time.

• Show the flashcards of the new words to establish meaning as an additional visual aid.

• Teach new words with most familiar songs or melodies. For example, when teaching "stand up and sit down", the teacher can sing "stand up and sit down" repeatedly with the "Ten little Indians" melody.

• Use fun activities to help students memorize new words in a low anxiety atmosphere. For example, when teaching the word "bite", ask students to walk around a circle or walk like an animal in the classroom by saying "bite".

Ways to teach story

• Prepare question word cards with Pinyin and English meaning when asking questions. When asking a question, point to the question word to establish the meaning every time.

• Introduce the main characters. e.g. He is Tom. She is Nini. Then ask students what the main characters' names are.

• Start the story from the cover. When asking questions to students, point to the question word to provide clear meaning every time. e.g. What does she say? Who is singing? Is he singing or is she dancing?

• In the middle of the story use 5-wh question words to develop or to bed the story.

• Let students predict the ending. e.g. Who feels hurt? The brother or the sister?

• Sometimes create a pause or wait time to let students finish the sentence or for a tense moment.

• Use sounds and visual tools. Capture students' attention with surprise sound effects. For example, when the students need to say "wow", teach them to use funny sound effect for "wow".

• Maintain eye contact. It will draw students' attention when the teacher makes eye contact with them.

• Use multiple ways of movement. For example, when the students hear the new words such as "be quiet", they need to show "quiet" gesture. As the storyteller, the teacher can "paint" pictures with his / her hands, feet, legs and head.

• Change your voice with different characters. Voice is one of the best ways to bring the character to life and gets students' attention immediately.

• Use props. Don't introduce the props all at once, but bring them out one by one during poignant parts in the telling.

Ways to teach song

• Slow & body movements are the key methods to teach song.

• First of all, let students listen to the melody by demonstrating with body movement.

• The teacher demonstrates singing the song line by line slowly.

• Invite students as a song leader to guide others for singing.

• Sing fast or slow, higher or lower for fun. Let students sing very slowly or sing faster each time to exaggerate the tempo.

• Humming the song. When students are familiar with the song, let them hum the song, which make the song more attractive for them to sing.

• Magic claps or stamp feet. When hearing assigned words, students need to clap hands or "be quiet" or stamp feet. After couple time of practices, then have a competition.

• Play games when singing a song.

Ways to teach games

- Games are played in very class period as a review for the language.
- Model the game before it starts. Invite one or two students to demonstrate how to play the game.
- Explain teacher's expectations before the games.
- Prepare the props or flashcards beforehand for the games.

How to use activities

- Activities are designed to reinforce students' speaking and listening skills.
- Model before starting the activity.
- Prepare the activities with diversified requirements to achieve the maximum benefit of the activity.
- Provide students with more practice in the process by having them share the answers with their partners before answering the class.

Ways to retell a story / do a role play

- Pair up students to retell the story with the retelling page.
- Pair up students. When a student describes the picture randomly, another one points to the picture accordingly.
- Invite students to act out the story either with props or character cards.
- Let students use props or a stage theater to retell the story or do a role play which help some students who are shy to present in low anxiety.

How to use word list

Students themselves can use the word list to review and monitor what they have learned after class. The teacher can use it to check if the students have mastered the words or not. A better way of checking is to combine the word list with flashcards. For example, students should find the correct flashcard when the teacher says a word at random.

Contents

夏天来了
Summer is here

故事简介

夏天来了，Alan 一家去海边度假。Alan 忍受不了炎热的天气，游泳后吃了很多西瓜，又喝了冰水和果汁。在 Alan 感觉很爽的时候发生了什么呢?

教学目标

1.掌握食物词语"冰水""西瓜"。
2.掌握季节词语"夏天"。

主要人物

Alan　　妈妈　　爸爸

哥哥　　姐姐　　妹妹

生词教学

• **夏天**

1.领读。（展示图片。）

2.观看视频 ▶，说一说视频中是什么季节。

3.老师准备不同季节的图片。学生看到"夏天"时，大拇指向上指，并大声说出生词。如果不是"夏天"，大拇指向下指。

4.借助课本 P12 的活动，让学生两人一组完成练习，说一说夏天可以做什么、穿什么，天气怎么样。

• **西瓜**

1.领读。（展示图片。）

2.观看视频 ▶，说一说视频中是什么水果。

3.让学生画一画西瓜，说一说西瓜什么颜色，顺便带领学生复习学过的其他水果。

4.借助课本 P11 的活动，让学生两人一组完成练习。除了练习"西瓜"，还可以复习其他食物词。

• **冰水**

1.领读。（展示图片。）

2.老师准备冰水和常温的水，让同学摸一摸、说一说。

3.借助课本 P9 的歌曲练习词语。

4.借助课本 P10 的游戏练习词语。

New words

- 夏天
  summer

- 西瓜
  watermelon

- 冰水
  ice water

学过的词： 来了、真热、我、去、游泳、吃、我的、肚子

故事热身

提问

1. 他们是谁？（指着 Alan 一家人问。）
2. 今天天气怎么样？（让学生说一说。）
3. 这是什么？（指着西瓜问。）
4. 这是什么？（指着球问。）
5. 他们去做什么？（让学生猜一猜。）

小提示

1. 借助书中的人物图介绍故事主要人物：Alan、爸爸妈妈、兄弟姐妹。
2. 教师准备英文图卡解释可能用到的、学生没学过的词语。
3. 可以结合对版插画进行差异化教学，问学生不同的问题，例如为什么喜欢 / 不喜欢夏天。

Story

夏天来了。

提问

1. 现在是什么季节？（让学生说一说。）
2. 他们喜欢夏天吗？（指着 Alan 一家人问。）
3. 夏天可以吃什么？（指着妈妈手中的西瓜问。）
4. 夏天可以做什么？（让学生说一说。）
5. 他们在哪里？（指着 Alan 一家人问。）

小提示

提示学生注意爸爸手里的盒子，让学生猜一猜里边有什么。

提问

1. 天气热吗？（让学生说一说。）

2. Alan 去做什么？（指着 Alan 问。）

3. 你会游泳吗？（让学生说一说。）

提问

1. 他们吃什么？（指着 Alan 和家人问。）
2. 他们为什么吃西瓜？（指着 Alan 和家人问。）
3. 你喜欢吃西瓜吗？（让学生说一说。）
4. 西瓜好吃吗？（让学生说一说。）

小提示

提示学生注意 Alan 吃了几块西瓜，一起数一数。

提问

1. Alan 喝什么？（指着 Alan 问。）

2. Alan 为什么喝冰水？（指着 Alan 问。）

3. 哥哥喝果汁还是喝冰水？（指着 Alan 的哥哥问。）

4. 姐姐喝果汁还是喝冰水？（指着 Alan 的姐姐问。）

5. 你喜欢喝果汁还是冰水？（让学生说一说。）

小提示

提示学生观察姐姐手里拿的球，猜猜他们刚才做了什么。

提问

1. Alan 怎么了？（指着 Alan 问。）

2. Alan 为什么肚子疼？（让学生说一说。）

小提示

1. 引导学生回顾前面的情节，说一说 Alan 都吃了什么、喝了什么。

2. 提示学生数一数 Alan 喝了几瓶冰水、几瓶果汁。

冬天来了
Winter is here

故事简介

刮风了，树叶落了，天气冷了，小鸟们戴上了围巾和帽子。它们到处找朋友，但是朋友们都要冬眠了。天空下起了雪，冬天来了。

教学目标

1. 掌握结构"我要……了"。
2. 掌握天气词语"下雪"。
3. 掌握季节词语"冬天"。

主要人物

小鸟

乌龟

青蛙

松鼠

生词教学

• 我要……了

1. 领读。（动作演示。）

2. 准备一些情景图片（看书、洗澡、睡觉等），让学生随机抽取图片，然后拿着抽到的图片，告诉 5 个同学"我要……了"。

3. 借助课本 P24 的活动练习词语。老师也可以跨学科教学，向学生介绍哪些动物冬眠。

• 下雪

1. 领读。（展示图片。）

2. 观看视频 ▶ ，让学生说一说视频中是什么天气。

3. 借助课本 P22 的游戏练习词语。

• 冬天

1. 领读。（展示图片。）

2. 观看视频 ▶ ，让学生说一说视频中是什么季节。

3. 借助课本 P21 的歌曲练习词语，顺便带领学生复习其他季节词。

小提示

准备一些国家的四季的图片，让学生说一说图片上的国家是什么季节。

New words

- 我要……了
  I'm going to...
- 下雪
  snow
- 冬天
  winter

学过的词： 我、很冷、睡觉、来了

故事热身

提问

1. 有几只小鸟？（指着小鸟问，让学生数一数。）

2. 小鸟戴着什么？它们冷吗？（指着小鸟问。）

3. 树叶什么颜色？它们怎么了？（指着飘落的树叶问。）

小提示

1. 借助书中的人物图介绍故事主要动物：小鸟、乌龟、青蛙和松鼠。

2. 教师准备英文图卡解释可能用到的、学生没学过的词语。

3. 提示学生注意图片，让学生猜一猜树叶为什么落了。

提问

1. 小鸟要做什么？（指着小鸟问。）

2. 它是谁？（指着乌龟问。）

3. 乌龟怎么了？（指着乌龟问，让学生注意乌龟的表情。）

4. 乌龟要做什么？（指着乌龟问。）

提问

1. 它是谁？（指着青蛙问。）

2. 青蛙怎么了？（指着青蛙问，让学生注意青蛙的表情。）

3. 青蛙要做什么？（指着青蛙问。）

提问

1. 它是谁？（指着松鼠问，让学生猜一猜。）

2. 松鼠也要睡觉了吗？（指着松鼠问。）

3. 树叶为什么落了？（指着树叶问，让学生猜一猜。）

小提示

1. 教师可以准备图片，介绍需要冬眠的动物。

2. 引导学生回顾前面的情节，说一说乌龟、青蛙和松鼠为什么要睡觉了。

3. 提示学生注意飘落的树叶的颜色，让学生说一说树叶为什么落了。

提问

1. 天气冷吗？（指着图片问。）

2. 小鸟为什么很高兴？（指着小鸟问。）

3. 小鸟喜欢下雪吗？（让学生说一说。）

4. 你喜欢下雪吗？（让学生说一说。）

提问

1.什么季节来了？（指着雪花问。）

2.冬天来了，要穿什么？你可以做什么？（让学生说一说。）

3.四个季节中，你最喜欢哪个季节？（让学生说一说。）

Lesson 3
下雨了
It's rainy

故事简介

Jenny 的姐姐、哥哥和小狗在院子里玩儿飞盘。不断有"雨滴"落下来，姐姐和哥哥以为下雨了，但其实……

教学目标

掌握天气词语"下雨""晴天"。

主要人物

Jenny

姐姐

哥哥

弟弟

生词教学

- **下雨**

1. 领读。（展示图片。）
2. 观看视频 ，让学生说一说视频中是什么天气。
3. 借助课本 P35 的活动练习词语。

- **晴天**

1. 领读。（展示图片。）
2. 借助课本 P36 的活动练习词语。

故事热身

提问

1. 哥哥和姐姐在玩儿什么？你们玩儿过飞盘吗？好玩儿吗？（让学生说一说。）

2. 弟弟去哪里？（指着弟弟问。）

3. 今天天气怎么样？（让学生说一说，让学生注意阳台上的花。）

小提示

1. 借助书中的人物图介绍故事主要人物：Jenny、哥哥、姐姐和弟弟。

2. 教师准备英文图卡解释可能用到的、学生没学过的词语。

3. 提示学生注意观察图片，让学生说一说楼上阳台的花什么颜色。

提问

1. 姐姐说什么？（指着姐姐问。）

2. 雨大吗？（指着雨滴问。）

下雨了。

提问

雨大吗? (指着雨滴问。)

小提示

提示学生注意雨滴。

提问

1. 现在下雨吗？（指着图片问。）
2. 你喜欢什么天气？（让学生说一说。）

小提示

借助课本 P36 的活动做练习，让学生说一说晴天可以做什么户外活动。

提问

1. 雨大吗？（指着雨滴问。）
2. Jenny 喜欢下雨吗？（指着 Jenny 问。）

小提示

1. 提示学生注意哥哥和姐姐的表情，让学生猜一猜他们想说什么。
2. 引导学生回顾前面的情节，让学生猜一猜为什么会下雨，发生了什么。

提问

1. Jenny、哥哥、姐姐和小狗看什么？（指着 Jenny、哥哥、姐姐和小狗问。）

2. 弟弟说什么？他为什么这样说？（指着弟弟问。）

3. 弟弟刚刚做什么了？（让学生说一说。）

4. 所以，今天是什么天气？下雨了吗？（让学生说一说。）

小提示

1. 提示学生注意 Jenny、哥哥、姐姐和小狗的表情，让学生猜一猜他们想说什么。

2. 引导学生回顾故事情节，让学生说一说到底发生了什么。

刮风了
It's windy

故事简介

John、Tom 和 Henry 在客厅里。John 望着窗外，Tom 坐着看书，Henry 躺在沙发上睡着了。外面刮风了，不一会儿又下雨了，John 高兴地冒雨跑出去玩儿，结果⋯⋯

教学目标

1. 掌握天气词语"刮风"。
2. 掌握身体名词"头发"。
3. 掌握状态词语"湿了"。
4. 掌握疾病词语"感冒"。

主要人物

John

Tom

Henry

奶奶

生词教学

• **刮风**

1. 领读。（展示图片。）

2. 观看视频 ，让学生说一说视频中是什么天气。

3. 借助课本 P45 的歌曲练习词语。

• **头发**

1. 领读。（展示图片或实物。）

2. 你的头发什么颜色？（让学生说一说。）

3. 借助课本 P46 的游戏练习词语。

• **湿了**

1. 领读。（展示图片。）

2. 观看视频 ，让学生说一说视频中的人物怎么了。

3. 借助课本 P48 的活动练习词语。

New words

- 刮风
  windy
- 头发
  hair
- 湿了
  get wet
- 感冒
  have a cold

学过的词：你、下雨

- **感冒**

1. 领读。（展示图片或动作演示。）

2. 观看视频 ▶，让学生说一说视频中的人物怎么了。

3. 借助课本 P47 的活动练习词语。

故事热身

提问

1. 他们是谁？他们在做什么？（指着 John、Tom 和 Henry 问。）

2. 猜一猜 John 在看什么？（指着 John 问。）

3. 小狗怎么了？（指着小狗问。）

4. Henry 手里拿着什么？（指着 Henry 问。）

5. 墙上挂着谁的照片？（指着墙上的照片问。）

小提示

1. 借助书中的人物图介绍故事主要人物：John、Tom、Henry 和奶奶。

2. 教师准备英文图卡解释可能用到的、学生没学过的词语。

3. 提示学生注意观察客厅里的摆设，让学生说一说客厅里有什么。

提问

1. 今天天气怎么样？（指着窗外问。）
2. John 喜欢刮风吗？（指着 John 问。）

小提示

提示学生注意小狗的表情，让学生说一说小狗喜不喜欢刮风。

32

下雨了。

提问

1. 现在天气怎么样？（指着图片问。）
2. John 喜欢下雨吗？（指着 John 问。）
3. 你喜欢下雨吗？下雨天你做什么？（让学生说一说。）

小提示

提示学生注意 Tom 和小狗的表情，让学生说一说他们喜不喜欢下雨，猜一猜他们想说什么。

提问

John 的头发怎么了？（指着 John 问。）

提问

1. 谁说"哎呀"？（指着 Tom 和 Henry 问。）
2. Tom 和 Henry 为什么说"哎呀"？（让学生猜一猜。）

小提示

提示学生注意 Tom、Henry 和小狗的表情，让学生猜一猜他们为什么说"哎呀"。

提问

1. 谁感冒了？（指着 John 问。）

2. 你们谁感冒了？（让学生说一说。）

3. 感冒了怎么办？（让学生说一说。）

小提示

1. 提示学生注意奶奶、Tom、Henry 和小狗的表情，让学生说一说他们想对 John 说什么。

2. 引导学生回顾故事情节，让学生说一说 John 为什么感冒了，感冒了怎么办。